For Korah

G. P. PUTNAM'S SONS
An imprint of Penguin Random House LLC, New York

First published in the United States of America by G. P. Putnam's Sons,
an imprint of Penguin Random House LLC, 2022

Visit us online at penguinrandomhouse.com

Library of Congress Cataloging-in-Publication Data
Names: Marcero, Deborah, author, illustrator.
Title: Out of a jar / Deborah Marcero.
Description: New York: G. P. Putnam's Sons, 2022. | Summary: Llewellyn, a little rabbit
overwhelmed by his emotions, hides away his feelings in glass jars, until he discovers life is more
colorful when he sets his emotions free.
Identifiers: LCCN 2021001739 (print) | LCCN 2021001740 (ebook) | ISBN 9780593326374
(hardcover) | ISBN 9780593326381 (epub) | ISBN 9780593326398 (kindle edition)
Subjects: CYAC: Rabbits—Fiction. | Emotions—Fiction.
Classification: LCC PZ7.1.M3699 Ou 2022 (print) | LCC PZ7.1.M3699 (ebook) | DDC [E]—dc23
LC record available at https://lccn.loc.gov/2021001739
LC ebook record available at https://lccn.loc.gov/2021001740

Manufactured in Spain

ISBN 9780593326374

10 9 8 7 6 5 4 3 2 1
EST

Design by Eileen Savage | Text set in Tuff Normal
The art was done with watercolor, pencil, colored pencils, ink, and digital media.

OUT OF A JAR

DEBORAH MARCERO

G. P. PUTNAM'S SONS

Llewellyn loved scary books,

scary jokes,

and scary cartoons.

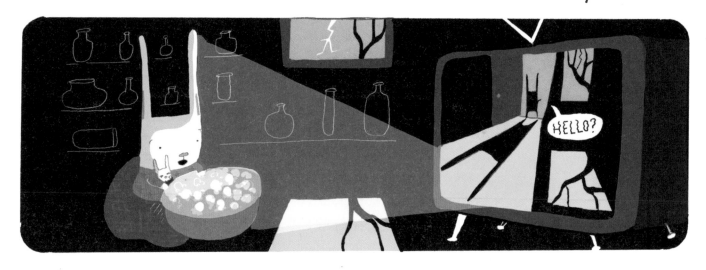

But Llewellyn did *not* like to be scared.

He tried to put the feeling away.

Here.

Then there.

But no matter what he did,

it kept coming back.

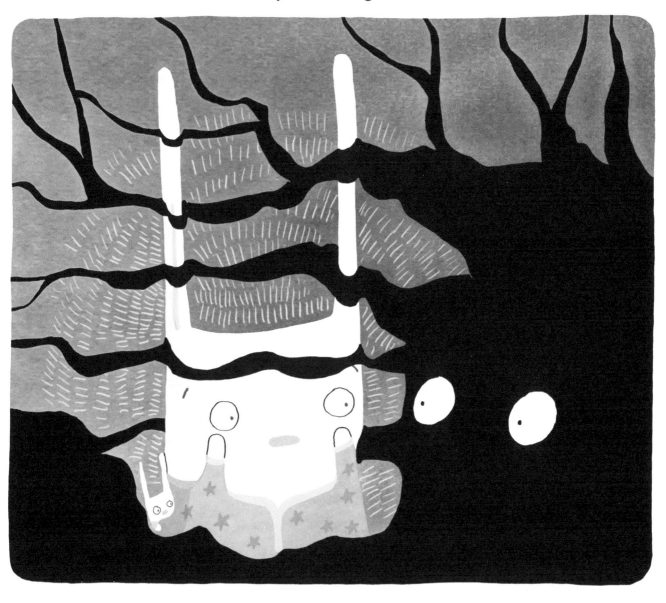

Finally, Llewellyn put his fear in a jar
and found a place to lock it away.

There it stayed. He didn't feel afraid anymore.

And that was that.

Not long after,
Llewellyn felt sad.

His best friend, Max,
was laughing and sharing
secrets without him.

Don't be glum.
Cheer up!

someone
said.

So he put his sadness in a jar too.

He locked it away,

and that was that.

Then, during music class, he got SO EXCITED!

But he wasn't supposed to dance. He was supposed to listen.

So he shoved
his excitement
in a jar too.

And that was that.

Anger.

Loneliness.

Joy.

Disappointment.

He put them all in jars.

And that . . .   and that . . .   and that . . .   was that!

Soon, he had so many jars
 filled with so many emotions
  that Llewellyn walked around . . .

not feeling much of anything at all.

One day, Llewellyn was feeling inspired.

But Max pointed and squealed with laughter.

Llewellyn was so embarrassed. He tried not to show it—

but that just made it worse.

Of course, Llewellyn knew just what to do.

He put his embarrassment in a jar.

But there was a problem. There was no more room.

Llewellyn tried to push and shove and shut his feelings away.

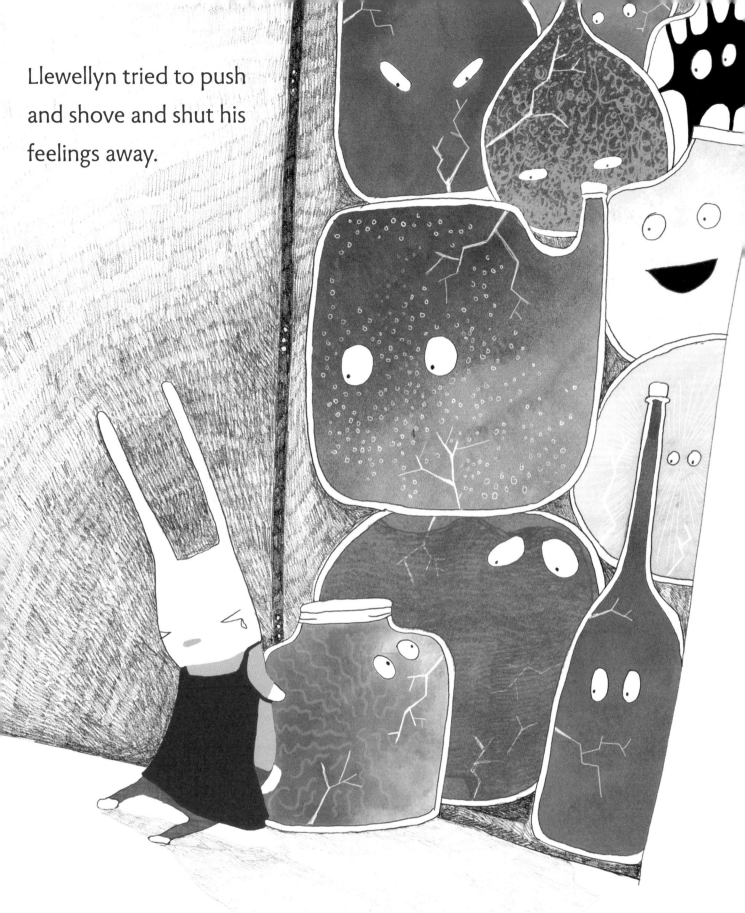

Tears of frustration leaked out, and something rumbled deep inside of him.

RRAAAAACK!

all of those jars,
holding all of those feelings,
shattered.

Every single feeling broke loose and pummeled
Llewellyn with a stampede that turned him into
a ragged heap of bunny on the floor.

Buried at the bottom,
fear was the last to leave.

Once those feelings were out,
something happened that Llewellyn didn't expect.

He was happy and sad at the same time.
He was excited *and* worried.

But most of all, he felt relieved.

So in the future, whenever Llewellyn was

JUBILANT

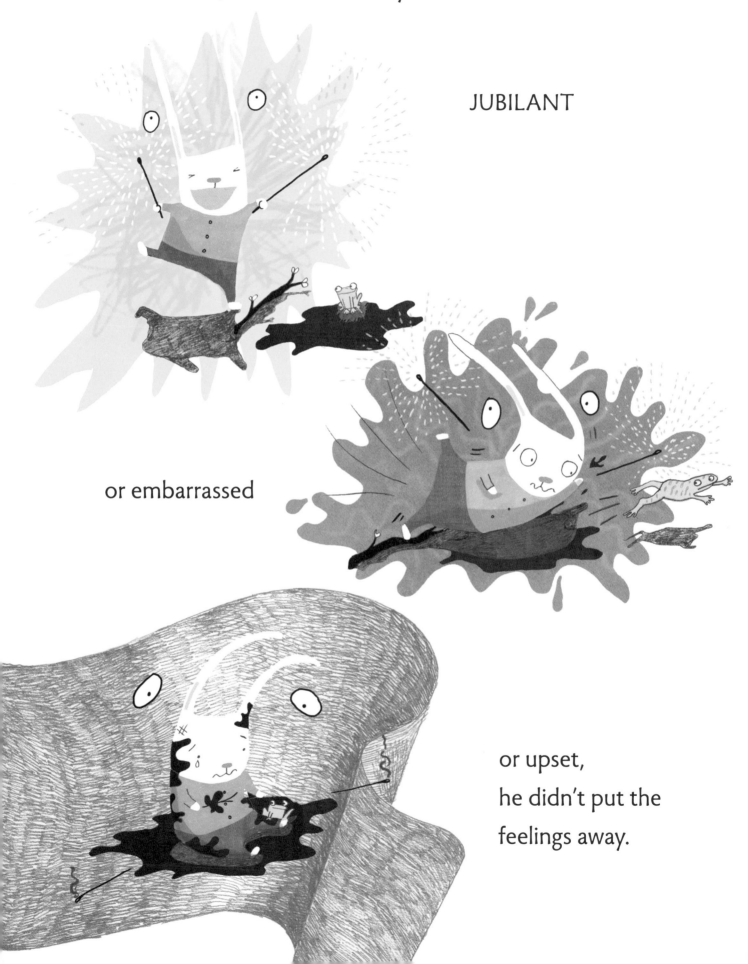

or embarrassed

or upset,
he didn't put the
feelings away.

Instead, he mustered up the courage to feel them.

To share them.

And, when he was ready,
to look each feeling in the eye,

give it a hug,

and let it go.

And that . . .

really was that.